‘“Oh, good God,” he kept saying with great relish. “Good God . . .”’

ANTON CHEKHOV

Born 1860, Taganrog, Russia

Died 1904, Badenweiler, Germany

'The Kiss' was first published in 1887; 'The Two Volodyas' in 1893; and 'Gooseberries' in 1898. This selection has been taken from the three volumes of Chekhov's short stories available in Penguin Classics.

CHEKHOV IN PENGUIN CLASSICS

The Steppe and Other Stories, 1887–1891

Ward No. 6 and Other Stories, 1892–1895

The Lady with the Little Dog and Other Stories, 1896–1904

The Shooting Party

Plays

A Life in Letters

ANTON CHEKHOV

Gooseberries

Translated by
Ronald Wilks

PENGUIN BOOKS

PENGUIN CLASSICS

UK | USA | Canada | Ireland | Australia
India | New Zealand | South Africa

Penguin Books is part of the Penguin Random House group of companies
whose addresses can be found at global.penguinrandomhouse.com.

This selection published in Penguin Classics 2015
003

Set in 9/12.4 pt Baskerville 10 Pro
Typeset by Jouve (UK), Milton Keynes
Printed in Great Britain by Clays Ltd, St Ives plc

A CIP catalogue record for this book is available from the British Library

ISBN: 978-0-141-39709-2

www.greenpenguin.co.uk

Contents

The Kiss

On 20 May, at eight o'clock in the evening, all six batteries of a reserve artillery brigade, on their way back to headquarters, stopped for the night at the village of Mestechki. At the height of all the confusion – some officers were busy with the guns, while others had assembled in the main square by the churchyard fence to receive their billetings – someone in civilian dress rode up from behind the church on a strange horse: it was small and dun-coloured with a fine neck and short tail, and seemed to move sideways instead of straight ahead, making small dancing movements with its legs as if they were being whipped. When the rider came up to the officers he doffed his hat and said, 'Our squire, His Excellency, Lieutenant-General von Rabbeck, invites you for tea and would like you to come now . . .'

The horse performed a bow and a little dance, and retreated with the same sideways motion. The rider raised his hat again and quickly disappeared behind the church on his peculiar horse.

'To hell with it!' some of the officers grumbled as they rode off to their quarters. 'We want to sleep and up pops this von Rabbeck with his tea! We know what *that* means all right!'

Every officer in the six batteries vividly remembered the previous year when they were on manoeuvres with officers from a Cossack regiment and had received a similar invitation from a landowning count, who was a retired officer. This hospitable and genial count had plied them with food and drink, would not hear of them returning to their billets and made them stay the night. That was all very well, of course, and they could not have hoped for better. But the trouble was that this retired officer was overjoyed beyond measure at having young men as his guests and he regaled them with stories from his glorious past until dawn, led them on a tour of the house, showed them his valuable paintings, old engravings and rare guns, and read out signed letters from eminent personages; and all this time the tired and weary officers listened, looked, pined for bed, and continuously yawned in their sleeves. When their host finally let them go, it was too late for bed.

Now, was this von Rabbeck one of the same breed? Whether he was or not, there was nothing they could do about it. The officers put clean uniforms on, smartened themselves up and went off en masse to look for the squire's house. On the square by the church they were told that they could either take the lower path leading down to the river behind the church, and then go along the bank to the garden, or they could ride direct from the church along the higher road which would bring them to the count's barns about a quarter of a mile from the village. The officers decided on the higher route.

'Who is this von Rabbeck?' they argued as they rode along. 'Is he the one who commanded a cavalry division at Plevna?'

'No, that wasn't von Rabbeck, just Rabbe, and without the "von".'

'It's marvellous weather, anyway!'

The road divided when they reached the first barn: one fork led straight on and disappeared in the darkness of the evening, while the other turned towards the squire's house on the right. The officers took the right fork and began to lower their voices . . . Stone barns with red tiled roofs stood on both sides of the road and they had the heavy, forbidding look of some provincial barracks. Ahead of them were the lighted windows of the manor-house.

'That's a good sign, gentlemen!' one of the officers said. 'Our setter's going on in front. That means he scents game!'

Lieutenant Lobytko, a tall, strongly built officer, who was riding ahead of the others, who had no moustache (although he was over twenty-five there wasn't a trace of hair on his face), and who was renowned in the brigade for his keen senses and ability to sniff a woman out from miles away, turned round and said, 'Yes, there must be women here, my instinct tells me.'

The officers were met at the front door by von Rabbeck himself – a fine-looking man of about sixty, wearing civilian clothes. He said how very pleased and happy he was to see the officers as he shook hands, but begged them most sincerely, in the name of God, to excuse him for not inviting them to stay the night, as two sisters with their children, his brothers and some neighbours had turned up, and he didn't have one spare room.

The general shook everyone's hand, apologized and smiled, but they could tell from his face that he wasn't nearly as pleased to have guests as last year's count and he had only asked them as it was the done thing. And, as they climbed the softly carpeted stairs and listened, the officers sensed that they had been invited only because it would have caused embarrassment if they had *not* been invited. At the sight of footmen dashing around lighting the lamps in the hall and upstairs, they felt they had introduced a note of uneasiness and anxiety into the house. And how could any host be pleased at having nineteen strange officers descend on a house where two sisters, children, brothers and neighbours had already arrived, most probably to celebrate some family anniversary. They were met in the ballroom upstairs by a tall, stately old lady with black eyebrows and a long face – the living image of Empress Eugénie. She gave them a majestic, welcoming smile and said how glad and happy she was to have them as guests and apologized for the fact that she and her husband weren't able to invite the officers to stay overnight on this occasion. Her beautiful, majestic smile, which momentarily disappeared every time she turned away from her guests, revealed that in her day she had seen many officers, that she had no time for them now, and that she had invited them and was apologizing only because her upbringing and social position demanded it.

The officers entered the large dining-room where about ten gentlemen and ladies, old and young, were sitting along one side of the table having tea. Behind their chairs, enveloped in a thin haze of cigar smoke, was a group of men with a rather lean, young, red-whiskered man in the middle, rolling his 'r's as he spoke out loud in English. Behind them, through a door, was a bright room with light blue furniture.

'Gentlemen, there's so many of you, it's impossible to

introduce *everyone*!' the general was saying in a loud voice, trying to sound cheerful. 'So don't stand on ceremony, introduce yourselves!'

Some officers wore very serious, even solemn expressions; others forced a smile, and all of them felt awkward as they bowed rather indifferently and sat down to tea.

Staff-Captain Ryabovich, a short, stooping officer, with spectacles and lynx-like side whiskers, was more embarrassed than anyone else. While his fellow-officers were trying to look serious or force a smile, his face, lynx-like whiskers and spectacles seemed to be saying, 'I'm the shyest, most modest and most insignificant officer in the whole brigade!' When he first entered the dining-room and sat down to tea, he found it impossible to concentrate on any one face or object. All those faces, dresses, cut-glass decanters, steaming glasses, moulded cornices, merged into one composite sensation, making Ryabovich feel ill at ease, and he longed to bury his head somewhere. Like a lecturer at his first appearance in public, he could see everything in front of him well enough, but at the same time he could make little sense of it (physicians call this condition, when someone sees without understanding, 'psychic blindness'). But after a little while Ryabovich began to feel more at home, recovered his normal vision and began to take stock of his surroundings. Since he was a timid and unsociable person, he was struck above all by what he himself had never possessed – the extraordinary boldness of these unfamiliar people. Von Rabbeck, two elderly ladies, a young girl in a lilac dress, and the young man with red whiskers – Rabbeck's youngest son – had sat themselves very cunningly among the officers, as though it had all been rehearsed. Straight away they had launched into a heated argument, which the guests could not help joining. The girl in lilac very excitedly insisted that the artillery had a much easier time than either the cavalry or the infantry, while Rabbeck and the elderly ladies argued the contrary. A rapid conversational crossfire ensued. Ryabovich glanced at the lilac girl who was arguing so passionately about something that was so foreign to her, so utterly boring, and he could see artificial smiles flickering over her face.

Von Rabbeck and family skilfully drew the officers into the argument, at the same time watching their wine glasses with eagle eyes to check whether they were filled, that they had enough sugar, and one officer who wasn't eating biscuits or drinking any brandy worried them. The more Ryabovich looked and listened, the more he began to like this insincere but wonderfully disciplined family.

After tea the officers went into the ballroom. Lieutenant Lobytko's instinct had not failed him: the room was full of girls and young married women. Already this 'setter' lieutenant had positioned himself next to a young blonde in a black dress, bending over dashingly as though leaning on some invisible sabre, smiling and flirting with his shoulders. Most probably he was telling her some intriguing nonsense as the blonde glanced superciliously at his well-fed face and said, 'Really?'

If that 'setter' had had any brains, that cool 'Really?' should have told him that he would never be called 'to heel'.

The grand piano suddenly thundered out. The sounds of a sad waltz drifted through the wide-open windows and everyone remembered that outside it was spring, an evening in May, and they smelt the fragrance of the young leaves of the poplars, of roses and lilac. Ryabovich, feeling the effects of the brandy and the music, squinted at a window, smiled and watched the movements of the women. Now it seemed that the fragrance of the roses, the poplars and lilac wasn't coming from the garden but from the ladies' faces and dresses.

Rabbeck's son had invited a skinny girl to dance and waltzed twice round the room with her. Lobytko glided over the parquet floor as he flew up to the girl in lilac and whirled her round the room. They all began to dance . . . Ryabovich stood by the door with guests who were not dancing and watched. Not once in his life had he danced, not once had he put his arm round an attractive young woman's waist. He would usually be absolutely delighted when, with everyone looking on, a man took a young girl he hadn't met before by the waist and offered his shoulders for her to rest her hands on, but he could never imagine himself in that situation. There had been times when he envied his fellow-officers' daring and dashing ways and it made him very depressed. The realization that he was shy, round-shouldered, quite undistinguished, that he had a long waist, lynx-like side whiskers, hurt him deeply. But over the years this realization had become something of a habit and as he watched his friends dance or talk out loud he no longer envied them but was filled with sadness.

When the quadrille began, young von Rabbeck went over to the officers who were not dancing and invited two of them to a game of billiards. They accepted and left the great hall with him. As he had nothing else to do, and feeling he would like to take at least some part in what was going on, Ryabovich trudged off after them. First they went into the drawing-room, then down a narrow corridor with a glass ceiling, then into a room where three sleepy footmen leapt up from a sofa the moment they entered. Finally, after passing through a whole series of rooms, young Rabbeck and company reached a small billiard-room and the game began.

Ryabovich, who never played any games except cards, stood by the table and indifferently watched the players, cue in hand, walking up and down in their unbuttoned tunics, making puns and shouting things he could not understand. The players ignored him, only turning round to say, 'I beg your pardon', when one of them happened accidentally to nudge him with an elbow or prod him with a cue. Even before the first game was over, he was bored and began to feel he was not wanted, that he was in the way . . . He felt drawn back to the ballroom and walked away.

As he walked back he had a little adventure. Halfway, he realized he was lost – he knew very well he had to go by those three sleepy footmen, but already he had passed through five or six rooms and those footmen seemed to have vanished into thin air. He realized his mistake, retraced his steps a little and turned to the right, only to find himself in a small, dimly lit room he had not seen on the way to the billiard-room. He stood still for a minute or so, opened the first door he came to with determination and entered a completely dark room. Ahead of him he could see light coming through a crack in the door and beyond was the muffled sound of a sad mazurka. The windows here had been left open as they had in the ballroom and he could smell poplars, lilac and roses . . .

Ryabovich stopped, undecided what to do . . . Just then he was astonished to hear hurried footsteps, the rustle of a dress and a female voice whispering breathlessly, 'At last!' Two soft, sweet-smelling arms (undoubtedly a woman's) encircled his neck, a burning cheek pressed against his and at the same time there was the sound of a kiss. But immediately after the kiss the woman gave a faint cry and shrank backwards in disgust – that was how it seemed to Ryabovich.

He was on the point of crying out too and he rushed towards the bright chink in the door.

His heart pounded away when he was back in the hall and his hands trembled so obviously that he hastily hid them behind his back. At first he was tormented by shame and he feared everyone there knew he had just been embraced and kissed, and this made him hesitate and look around anxiously. But when he had convinced himself that everyone was dancing and gossiping just as peacefully as before, he gave himself up to a totally new kind of sensation, one he had never experienced before in all his life. Something strange was happening to him . . . his neck, which just a few moments ago had been embraced by sweet-smelling hands, seemed anointed with oil. And on his left cheek, just by his moustache, there was a faint, pleasant, cold, tingling sensation, the kind you get from peppermint drops and the more he rubbed the spot the stronger the tingling became. From head to heels he was overcome by a strange, new feeling which grew stronger every minute. He wanted to dance, speak to everyone, run out into the garden, laugh out loud. He completely forgot his stoop, his insignificant appearance, his lynx-like whiskers and 'vague appearance' (once he happened to hear some ladies saying this about him). When Rabbeck's wife went by he gave her such a broad, warm smile that she stopped and gave him a very searching look.

'I love this house so much!' he said, adjusting his spectacles.

The general's wife smiled and told him that the house still belonged to her father. Then she asked if his parents were still alive, how long he had been in the army, why he was so thin, and so on . . . When Ryabovich had replied, she moved on, leaving him smiling even more warmly and he began to think he was surrounded by the most wonderful people . . .

Mechanically, Ryabovich ate and drank everything he was offered at the dinner table, deaf to everything as he tried to find an explanation for what had just happened. It was a mysterious, romantic incident, but it wasn't difficult to explain. No doubt some girl or young married woman had a rendezvous with someone in that dark room, had waited for a long time, and then mistook Ryabovich for her hero in her nervous excitement. This was the most likely explanation, all the more so as Ryabovich had hesitated in the middle of the room, which made it look as though he were expecting someone . . .

'But who *is* she?' he thought as he surveyed the ladies' faces. 'She must be young, as old ladies don't have rendezvous. And intelligent – I could tell from the rustle of her dress, her smell, her voice.'

He stared at the girl in lilac and found her very attractive.

She had beautiful shoulders and arms, a clever face and a fine voice. As he gazed at her, Ryabovich wanted *her*, no one else, to be that mysterious stranger . . . But she gave a rather artificial laugh and wrinkled her long nose, which made her look old. Then he turned to the blonde in black. She was younger, simpler and less affected, with charming temples and she sipped daintily from her wine glass. Now Ryabovich wanted her to be the stranger. But he soon discovered that she had a featureless face and he turned to her neighbour . . . 'It's hard to say,' he wondered dreamily. 'If I could just take the lilac girl's shoulders and arms away, add the blonde's temples, then take those eyes away from the girl on Lobytko's left, *then*.' He merged them all into one, so that he had an image of the girl who had kissed him, the image he desired so much, but which he just could not find among the guests around the table.

After dinner the officers, well-fed and slightly tipsy by now, began to make their farewells and expressed their thanks. Once again the hosts apologized for not having them stay the night.

'Delighted, gentlemen, absolutely delighted,' the general was saying and this time he meant it – probably because people are usually more sincere and better-humoured saying goodbye to guests than welcoming them.

'Delighted! Glad to see you back any time, so don't stand on ceremony. Which way are you going? The higher road? No, go through the garden, it's quicker.'

The officers went into the garden, where it seemed very dark and quiet after the bright lights and the noise. They did not say a word all the way to the gate. They were half-drunk, cheerful and contented, but the darkness and the silence made them pause for thought. Probably they were thinking the same as Ryabovich: would they ever see the day when they would own a large house, have a family, a garden, when *they* too would be able to entertain people (however much of a pretence this might be), feed them well, make them drunk and happy?

As they went through the garden gate they all started talking at once and, for no apparent reason, laughed out loud. Now they were descending the path that led down to the river and then ran along the water's edge, weaving its way around the bushes, the little pools of water and the willows which overhung the river. The bank and the path were barely visible, and the far side was plunged in darkness. Here and there were reflections of the stars in the water, quivering and breaking up into little patches – the only sign that the river was flowing fast. All was quiet. Sleepy sandpipers called plaintively from the far bank and on the near side a nightingale in a bush poured out its song, ignoring the passing officers.

The men paused by the bush, touched it, but still the nightingale sang.

'That's a bird for you!' approving voices murmured. 'Here we are, right next to him and he doesn't take a blind bit of notice! What a rascal!'

The path finally turned upwards and came out on to the high road by the church fence. The officers were exhausted from walking up the hill and sat down for a smoke. On the far bank they could make out a dim red light and they tried to pass the time by guessing whether it was a camp fire, a light in a window, or something else . . . Ryabovich looked at it and imagined that the light was winking at him and smiling, as though it knew all about that kiss.

When he reached his quarters Ryabovich quickly undressed and lay on his bed. In the same hut were Lobytko and Lieutenant Merzlyakov, a gentle, rather quiet young man, who was considered well-educated in his own little circle. He was always reading the *European Herald* when he had the chance and took it with him everywhere. Lobytko undressed, paced up and down for a long time, with the expression of a dissatisfied man, and sent the batman for some beer.

Merzlyakov lay down, placed a candle near his pillow and immersed himself in the *European Herald*.

'Who *is* she?' Ryabovich wondered as he glanced at the grimy ceiling. His neck still felt as if it had been anointed with oil and he had that tingling sensation around his mouth – just like peppermint drops. He had fleeting visions of the lilac girl's shoulders and arms, the temples and truthful eyes of the blonde in black, waists, dresses, brooches. He tried to fix these visions firmly in his mind, but they kept dancing about, dissolving, flickering. When these visions vanished completely against that darkened background everyone has when he closes his eyes, he began to hear hurried steps, rustling dresses, the sound of a kiss and he was gripped by an inexplicable, overwhelming feeling of joy. Just as he was abandoning himself to it, he heard the batman come back and report that there wasn't any beer. Lobytko became terribly agitated and started pacing up and down again.

'Didn't I tell you he's an idiot?' he said, stopping first in front of Ryabovich, then Merzlyakov. 'A man must really be a blockhead and idiot to come back without any beer! The man's a rogue, eh?'

'Of course, you won't find any beer in this place,' Merzlyakov said without taking his eyes off the *European Herald*.

'Oh, do you really think so?' Lobytko persisted. 'Good God, put me on the moon and I'll find you beer and women right away! Yes, I'll go now and find some . . . Call me a scoundrel if I don't succeed!'

He slowly dressed and pulled on his high boots. Then he finished his cigarette in silence and left.

'Rabbeck, Grabbeck, Labbeck,' he muttered, pausing in the hall. 'I don't feel like going on my own, dammit! Fancy a little walk, Ryabovich?'

There was no reply, so he came back, slowly undressed and got into bed. Merzlyakov sighed, put the *European Herald* away and snuffed the candle.

'Hm,' Lobytko murmured as he puffed his cigarette in the dark.

Ryabovich pulled the blankets over his head, curled himself into a ball and tried to merge the visions fleeting through his mind into one fixed image. But he failed completely. Soon he fell asleep and his last waking thought was of someone caressing him and making him happy, of something absurd and unusual, but nonetheless exceptionally fine and joyful, that had entered his life. And his dreams centred around this one thought.

When he woke up, the sensation of oil on his cheek and the minty tingling near his lips had vanished, but the joy of yesterday still filled his heart. Delighted, he watched the window frames, gilded now by the rising sun, and listened intently to the street noises. Outside, just by the window, he could hear loud voices – Lebedetsky, Ryabovich's battery commander, who had just caught up with the brigade, was shouting at his sergeant – simply because he had lost the habit of talking softly.

'Is there anything else?' he roared.

'When they were shoeing yesterday, sir, someone drove a nail into Pigeon's hoof. The medical orderly put clay and vinegar on it and they're keeping the horse reined, away from the others. And artificer Artemyev got drunk yesterday and the lieutenant had him tied to the fore-carriage of an auxiliary field-gun.'

And the sergeant had more to report. Karpov had forgotten the new cords for the trumpets and the stakes for the tents, and the officers had spent the previous evening as guests of General von Rabbeck. During the conversation, Lebedetsky's head and red beard appeared at the window. He blinked his short-sighted eyes at the sleepy officers and bade them good morning.

'Everything all right?' he asked.

'One of the shaft-horses damaged its withers – it was the new collar,' Lobytko answered, yawning.

The commander sighed, pondered for a moment and said in a loud voice, 'I'm still wondering whether to pay Aleksandra a visit, I really ought to go and see how she is. Well, goodbye for now, I'll catch you up by evening.'

A quarter of an hour later the brigade moved off. As it passed the general's barns, Ryabovich looked to the right where the house was. The blinds were drawn in all the windows. Clearly, everyone was still asleep. And the girl who had kissed Ryabovich the day before was sleeping too. He tried to imagine her as she slept and he had a clear and distinct picture of the wide-open windows, the little green branches peeping into her bedroom, the morning freshness, the smell of poplars, lilac and roses, her bed and the chair with that dress which had rustled the day before lying over it, tiny slippers, a watch on the table. But the actual features of that face, that sweet, dreamy smile, exactly what was most characteristic of her, slipped through his imagination like mercury through the fingers. When he had ridden about a quarter of a mile, he looked back. The yellow church, the house, the river and garden were flooded in sunlight and the river, with its bright green banks and its waters reflecting the light blue sky and glinting silver here and there, looked very beautiful. Ryabovich took a last look at Mestechki and he felt so sad, as if he were saying farewell to what was very near and dear to him.

But there were only long-familiar, boring scenes ahead of him. On both sides of the road there were fields of young rye and buckwheat, where crows were hopping about. Ahead, all he could see was dust and the backs of soldiers' heads; and behind, the same dust, the same faces. The brigade was led by a vanguard of four soldiers bearing sabres and behind them rode the military choristers, followed by trumpeters. Every now and then, like torchbearers in a funeral cortège, the vanguard and singers ignored the regulation distance and pushed on far ahead. Ryabovich rode alongside the first field-gun of the fifth battery and he could see the other four in front. These long, ponderous processions formed by brigades on the move can strike civilians as very peculiar, an unintelligible muddle, and non-military people just cannot fathom why a single field-gun has to be escorted by so many soldiers, why it has to be drawn by so many horses all tangled up in such strange harness, as if it really was such a terrible, heavy object. But Ryabovich understood everything perfectly well and for that reason he found it all extremely boring. He had long known why a hefty bombardier always rides with the officer at the head of every battery and why he is called an outrider. Immediately behind this bombardier came the riders on the first, then the middle-section trace-horses. Ryabovich knew that the horses to the left were saddle-horses, while those on the right were auxiliary – all this was very boring. The horsemen were followed by two shaft-horses, one ridden by a horseman with yesterday's dust still on his back and who had a clumsy-looking, very comical piece of wood fixed to his right leg. Ryabovich knew what it was for and did not find it funny. All the riders waved their whips mechanically and shouted now and again. As for the field-gun, it was an ugly thing. Sacks of oats covered with tarpaulin lay on the fore-carriage and the gun itself was hung with kettles, kit-bags and little sacks: it resembled a small harmless animal which had been surrounded, for some reason, by men and horses. On the side sheltered from the wind a team of six strode along, swinging their arms. This gun was followed by more bombardiers, riders, shaft-horses and another field-gun – just as ugly and uninspiring as the first – lumbering along in the rear. After the second gun came a third, then a fourth with an officer riding alongside (there are six batteries to a brigade and four guns to a battery). The whole procession stretched about a quarter of a mile and ended with the baggage wagons, where a most likeable creature plodded thoughtfully along, his long-eared head drooping: this was Magar the donkey, brought from Turkey by a certain battery commander.

Ryabovich looked apathetically at all those necks and faces in front and behind. At any other time he would have dozed off, but now he was immersed in new, pleasant thoughts. When the brigade had first set off, he had tried to convince himself that the incident of the kiss was only some unimportant, mysterious adventure and that essentially it was trivial and too ridiculous for serious thought. But very quickly he waved logic aside and gave himself up to his dreams. First he pictured himself in von Rabbeck's drawing-room, sitting next to a girl who resembled both the girl in lilac and the blonde in black. Then he closed his eyes and imagined himself with another, completely strange girl, with very indeterminate features: in his thoughts he spoke to her, caressed her and leaned his head on her shoulder. Then he thought of war and separation, reunion, dinner with his wife and children . . .

'Brakes on!' rang out the command every time they went downhill. He shouted the command too, and feared that his own shouts would shatter his daydreams and bring him back to reality.

As they passed some estate, Ryabovich peeped over the fence into the garden. There he saw a long avenue, straight as a ruler, strewn with yellow sand and lined with young birches. With the eagerness of a man who has surrendered himself to daydreaming, he imagined tiny female feet walking over the yellow sand. And, quite unexpectedly, he had a clear mental picture of the girl who had kissed him, the girl he had visualized the previous evening during dinner. This image had planted itself in his mind and would not leave him.

At midday someone shouted from a wagon in the rear, 'Attention, eyes left! Officers!'

The brigadier drove up in an open carriage drawn by two white horses. He ordered it to stop near the second battery and shouted something no one understood. Several officers galloped over to him, Ryabovich among them.

'Well, what's the news?' asked the brigadier, blinking his red eyes. 'Anyone ill?'

When they had replied, the brigadier, a small skinny man, chewed for a moment, pondered and then turned to one of the officers: 'One of your drivers, on the third gun, has taken his knee-guard off and the devil's hung it on the fore-carriage. Reprimand him!'

He looked up at Ryabovich and continued: 'It strikes me your harness breeches are too long.'

After a few more tiresome comments, the brigadier glanced at Lobytko and grinned. 'You look down in the dumps today, Lieutenant Lobytko. Pining for Madame Lopukhov, eh? Gentlemen, he's pining for Madame Lopukhov!'

Madame Lopukhov was a very plump, tall lady, well past forty. The brigadier, who had a passion for large women, no matter what age, suspected his officers nurtured similar passions. They smiled politely. Then the brigadier, delighted with himself for having made a very amusing, cutting remark, roared with laughter, tapped his driver on the back and saluted. The carriage drove off.

'All the things I'm dreaming about now and which seem impossible, out of this world, are in fact very ordinary,' Ryabovich thought as he watched the clouds of dust rising in the wake of the brigadier's carriage. 'It's all so very ordinary, everyone experiences it . . . The brigadier, for example. He was in love once, now he's married, with children. Captain Vachter is married and loved, despite having an extremely ugly red neck and no waistline. Salmanov is coarse and too much of a Tartar, but *he* had an affair that finished in marriage. I'm the same as everyone else . . . sooner or later I'll have to go through what they did . . .'

And he was delighted and encouraged by the thought that he was just an ordinary man, leading an ordinary life. Now he was bold enough to picture *her* and his happiness as much as he liked and he gave full rein to his imagination.

In the evening, when the brigade had reached its destination and the officers were resting in their tents, Ryabovich, Merzlyakov and Lobytko gathered round a trunk and had supper. Merzlyakov took his time, holding his *European Herald* on his knees and reading it as he slowly munched his food.

Lobytko could not stop talking and kept filling his glass with beer, while Ryabovich, whose head was rather hazy from dreaming all day long, said nothing as he drank. Three glasses made him tipsy and weak and he felt an irrepressible longing to share his new feelings with his friends.

'A strange thing happened to me at the Rabbecks,' he

said, trying to sound cool and sarcastic. 'I went to the billiard-room, you know . . .'

He began to tell them, in great detail, all about the kiss, but after a minute fell silent. In that one minute he had told them everything and he was astonished when he considered how little time was needed to tell his story: he had imagined it would take until morning. After he heard the story, Lobytko – who was a great liar and therefore a great sceptic – looked at him in disbelief and grinned. Merzlyakov twitched his eyebrows and kept his eyes glued to the *European Herald* as he calmly remarked, 'Damned if I know what to make of it! Throwing herself round a stranger's neck without saying a word first . . . She must have been a mental case . . .'

'Yes, some kind of neurotic,' Ryabovich agreed.

'Something similar happened to me once,' Lobytko said, assuming a frightened look. 'Last year I was travelling to Kovno . . . second class. The compartment was chock-full and it was impossible to sleep. So I tipped the guard fifty copeks . . . he took my luggage and got me a berth in a sleeper. I lay down and covered myself with a blanket. It was dark, you understand. Suddenly someone was touching my shoulder and breathing into my face. So I moved my arm and felt an elbow. I opened my eyes and – can you imagine! – it was a woman. Black eyes, lips as red as the best salmon, nostrils breathing passion, breasts like buffers! . . .'

'Just a minute,' Merzlyakov calmly interrupted. 'I don't dispute what you said about her breasts, but how could you see her lips if it was dark?'

Lobytko tried to wriggle out by poking fun at Merzlyakov's

obtuseness and this jarred on Ryabovich. He went away from the trunk, lay down and vowed never again to tell his secrets.

Camp life fell back into its normal routine. The days flashed by, each exactly the same as the other. All this time Ryabovich felt, thought and behaved like someone in love. When his batman brought him cold water in the mornings, he poured it over his head and each time he remembered that there was something beautiful and loving in his life.

In the evenings, when his fellow-officers talked about love and women, he would listen very attentively, sitting very close to them and assuming the habitual expression of a soldier hearing stories about battles he himself fought in. On those evenings when senior officers, led by 'setter' Lobytko, carried out 'sorties' on the local village, in true Don Juan style, Ryabovich went along with them and invariably returned feeling sad, deeply guilty and imploring *her* forgiveness. In his spare time, or on nights when he couldn't sleep, when he wanted to recall his childhood days, his parents, everything that was near and dear to him, he would always find himself thinking of Mestechki instead, of that strange horse, of von Rabbeck and his wife, who looked like the Empress Eugénie, of that dark room with the bright chink in the door.

On 31 August he left camp – not with his own brigade, however, but with two batteries. All the way he daydreamed and became very excited, as though he were going home. He wanted passionately to see that strange horse again, the church, those artificial Rabbecks, the dark room. Some inner voice, which so often deceives those in love, whispered that he was *bound* to see her again. And he was tormented by such questions as: how could he arrange a meeting, what would she say, had she forgotten the kiss? If the worst came to the worst, he would at least have the pleasure of walking through that dark room and remembering . . .

Towards evening, that familiar church and the white barns appeared on the horizon. His heart began to pound. He did not listen to what the officer riding next to him was saying, he was oblivious of everything and looked eagerly at the river gleaming in the distance, at the loft above which pigeons were circling in the light of the setting sun.

As he rode up to the church and heard the quartermaster speaking, he expected a messenger on horseback to appear from behind the fence any minute and invite the officers to tea . . . but the quartermaster read the billeting list out, the officers dismounted and strolled off into the village – and no messenger came.

'The people in the village will tell Rabbeck we're here and he'll send for us,' Ryabovich thought as he went into his hut. He just could not understand why a fellow-officer was lighting a candle, why the batmen were hurriedly heating the samovars.

He was gripped by an acute feeling of anxiety. He lay down, then got up and looked out of the window to see if the messenger was coming. But there was no one. He lay down again but got up again after half an hour, unable to control his anxiety, went out into the street and strode off towards the church.

The square near the fence was dark and deserted. Some soldiers were standing in a row at the top of the slope, saying nothing. They jumped when they saw Ryabovich and saluted. He acknowledged the salute and went down the familiar path.

The entire sky over the far bank was flooded with crimson; the moon was rising. Two peasant women were talking loudly and picking cabbage leaves as they walked along the edge of a kitchen garden. Beyond the gardens were some dark huts. On the near bank everything was much the same as in May: the path, the bushes, the willows overhanging the river . . . only there was no bold nightingale singing, no fragrant poplars or young grass. Ryabovich reached the garden and peered over the gate. It was dark and quiet and all he could see were the white trunks of the nearest birches and here and there little patches of avenue – everything else had merged into one black mass. Ryabovich looked hard, listened eagerly, and after standing and waiting for about a quarter of an hour, without hearing a sound or seeing a single light, he trudged wearily away . . .

He went down to the river, where he could see the general's bathing-hut and towels hanging over the rail on the little bridge. He went on to the bridge, stood for a moment and aimlessly fingered the towels. They felt cold and rough. He looked down at the water . . . the current was swift and purled, barely audibly, against the piles of the hut. The red moon was reflected in the water near the left bank; tiny waves rippled through the reflection, pulling it apart and breaking it up into little patches, as if trying to bear it away.

'How stupid, how very stupid!' Ryabovich thought as he looked at the fast-flowing water. Now, when he hoped for nothing, that adventure of the kiss, his impatience, his vague longings and disillusionment appeared in a new light. He didn't think it at all strange that he hadn't waited for the general's messenger or that he would never see the girl who had kissed him by mistake. On the contrary, he would have thought it strange if he *had* seen her . . .

The water raced past and he did not know where or why; it had flowed just as swiftly in May, when it grew from a little stream into a large river, flowed into the sea, evaporated and turned into rain. Perhaps this was the same water flowing past. To what purpose?

And the whole world, the whole of life, struck Ryabovich as a meaningless, futile joke. As he turned his eyes from the water to the sky, he remembered how fate had accidentally caressed him – in the guise of an unknown woman. He recalled the dreams and visions of that summer and his life seemed terribly empty, miserable, colourless . . . When he returned to his hut, none of the officers was there.

The batman reported that they had all gone to 'General Fontryabkin's' – he'd sent a messenger on horseback with the invitation. There was a brief flicker of joy in his heart, but he snuffed it out at once, lay on his bed and in defiance of fate – as though he wanted to bring its wrath down on his own head – he did not go to the general's.

The Two Volodyas

'Let me go, *I* want to drive. I'm going to sit next to the driver,' Sophia Lvovna shouted. 'Driver, wait. I'm coming up on to the box to sit next to you.'

She stood on the sledge while her husband Vladimir Nikitych and her childhood friend Vladimir Mikhaylych held her by the arm in case she fell. Away sped the troika.

'I said you shouldn't have given her brandy,' Vladimir Nikitych whispered irritably to his companion. 'You're a fine one!'

From past experience the Colonel knew that when women like his wife Sophia Lvovna had been in riotous, rather inebriated high spirits he could normally expect fits of hysterical laughter and tears to follow. He was afraid that once they got home he would have to run around with the cold compresses and medicine instead of being able to go to bed.

'Whoa!' Sophia Lvovna shouted. 'I want to drive.'

She was really very gay and in an exultant mood. For two months after her wedding she had been tormented by the thought that she had married Colonel Yagich for his money or, as they say, *par dépit*. That same evening, in the out-of-town restaurant, she finally became convinced that she loved him passionately. In spite of his fifty-four years, he was so trim, sprightly and athletic, and he told puns and joined in the gypsy girls' songs with such charm. It is true that nowadays old men are a thousand times more interesting than young ones, as though age and youth had changed places. The Colonel was two years older than her father, but was that important if, to be quite honest, he was infinitely stronger, more energetic and livelier than she was, even though she was only twenty-three?

'Oh, my darling!' she thought. 'My wonderful man!'

In the restaurant she had come to the conclusion too that not a spark remained of her old feelings. To her childhood friend Vladimir Mikhaylych, whom only yesterday she had loved to distraction, she now felt completely indifferent. The whole evening he had struck her as a lifeless, sleepy, boring nobody and the habitual coolness with which he avoided paying restaurant bills exasperated her so much this time that she very nearly told him, 'You should have stayed at home if you're so poor.' The Colonel footed the bill.

Perhaps it was the trees, telegraph poles and snowdrifts all flashing past that aroused the most varied thoughts. She reflected that the meal had cost one hundred and twenty roubles – with a hundred for the gypsies – and that the next day, if she so wished, she could throw a thousand roubles away, whereas two months ago, before the wedding, she did not have three roubles to call her own and she had to turn to her father for every little thing. How her life had changed!

Her thoughts were in a muddle and she remembered how, when she was about ten, Colonel Yagich, her husband now, had made advances to her aunt and how everyone in the house had said that he had ruined her. In fact, her aunt often came down to dinner with tear-stained eyes and was always going away somewhere; people said the poor woman was suffering terribly. In those days he was very handsome and had extraordinary success with women; the whole town knew him and he was said to visit his admirers every day, like a doctor doing his rounds. Even now, despite his grey hair, wrinkles and spectacles, his thin face looked handsome, especially in profile.

Sophia Lvovna's father was an army doctor and had once served in Yagich's regiment. Volodya senior's father had also been an army doctor and had once served in the same regiment as her own father and Yagich. Despite some highly involved and frantic amorous adventures Volodya junior had been an excellent student. He graduated with honours from university, had decided to specialize in foreign literature and was said to be writing his thesis. He lived in the barracks with his doctor father and he had no money of his own, although he was now thirty. When they were children, Sophia Lvovna and he had lived in different flats, but in the same building, and he often came to play with her; together they had dancing and French lessons. But when he grew up into a well-built, exceedingly good-looking young man, she began to be shy of him. Then she fell madly in love with him and was still in love until shortly before she married Yagich. He too had extraordinary success with women, from the age of fourteen almost, and the ladies who deceived their husbands with him exonerated themselves by saying Volodya was 'so little'. Not long before, he was said to be living in digs close to the university and every time you knocked, his footsteps could be heard on the other side of the door and then the whispered apology: '*Pardon, je ne suis pas seul.*' Yagich was delighted with him, gave him his blessing for the future as Derzhavin had blessed Pushkin, and was evidently very fond of him. For hours on end they would silently play billiards or piquet, and if Yagich went off somewhere in a troika, he would take Volodya with him; only Yagich shared the secret of his thesis. In earlier days, when the Colonel was younger, they were often rivals, but were never jealous of one another. When they were in company, which they frequented together, Yagich was called 'Big Volodya' and his friend 'Little Volodya'.

Besides Big Volodya and Little Volodya, and Sophia Lvovna, there was someone else in the sledge, Margarita Aleksandrovna – or Rita as everyone called her – Mrs Yagich's cousin. She was a spinster, in her thirties, very pale, with black eyebrows, pince-nez, who chain-smoked even when it was freezing; there was always ash on her lap and chest. She spoke through her nose and drawled; she was cold and unemotional, could drink any quantity of liqueur or brandy without getting drunk and told stories abounding in *doubles entendres* in a dull, tasteless way. At home she read the learned reviews all day long, scattering ash all over them; or she would eat crystallized apples.

'Sophia, don't play the fool,' she drawled; 'it's really so stupid.'

When the town gates came into view the troika slowed down; they caught glimpses of people and houses, and Sophia quietened down, snuggled against her husband and gave herself up to her thoughts. And now gloomy thoughts began to mingle with her happy, carefree fantasies. The man opposite knew that she had loved him (so she thought), and of course he believed the reports that she had married the

Colonel *par dépit*. Not once had she confessed her love and she did not want him to know. She had concealed her feelings, but his expression clearly showed that he understood her perfectly, and so her pride suffered. But most humiliating of all about her situation was the fact that Little Volodya had suddenly started paying attention to her after her marriage, which had never happened before. He would sit with her for hours on end, in silence, or telling her some nonsense; and now in the sledge he was gently touching her leg or squeezing her hand, without saying a word. Evidently, all he wanted was for her to get married. No less obviously, he did not think much of her and she interested him only in a certain way, as an immoral, disreputable woman. And this mingling of triumphant love for her husband and injured pride was the reason for her behaving so irresponsibly, prompting her to sit on the box and shout and whistle . . .

Just as they were passing the convent the great twenty-ton bell started clanging away. Rita crossed herself.

'Our Olga is in that convent,' Sophia Lvovna said, crossing herself and shuddering.

'Why did she become a nun?' the Colonel asked.

'*Par dépit*,' Rita answered angrily, obviously hinting at Sophia Lvovna's marriage to Yagich. 'This *par dépit* is all the rage now. It's a challenge to the whole of society. She was a proper good-time girl, a terrible flirt, all she liked was dances and dancing partners. And then suddenly we have all this! She took us all by surprise!'

'That's not true,' Little Volodya said, lowering the collar of his fur coat and revealing his handsome face. 'This wasn't a case of *par dépit*, but something really terrible. Her brother

Dmitry was sentenced to hard labour in Siberia and no one knows where he is now. The mother died of grief.' He raised his collar again. 'And Olga did the right thing,' he added dully. 'Living as a ward, and with a treasure like our Sophia Lvovna, what's more – that's enough food for thought!'

Sophia Lvovna noted the contempt in his voice and wanted to say something very nasty in reply, but she said nothing. Once more euphoria gripped her. She stood up and shouted tearfully, 'I want to go to morning service. Driver, turn back! I want to see Olga!'

They turned back. The convent bell had a dull peal and Sophia Lvovna felt there was something in it reminding her of Olga and her life. Bells rang out from other churches. When the driver had brought the troika to a halt, Sophia leapt from the sledge and rushed unescorted to the gates.

'Please don't be long!' her husband shouted. 'It's late.'

She went through the dark gates, then along the path leading to the main church; the light snow crunched under her feet and the tolling of the bells sounded right over her head now and seemed to penetrate her whole being. First she came to the church door, the three steps down, then the porch, with paintings of the saints on both sides; there was a smell of juniper and incense. Then came another door, which a dark figure opened, bowing very low . . . In the church the service had not yet begun. One of the nuns was in front of the icon-screen lighting candles in their holders, another was lighting a chandelier. Here and there, close to the columns and side-chapels, were motionless, black figures. 'They'll be standing in exactly the same places till morning,' Sophia Lvovna thought and the whole place struck her as dark, cold, depressing – more depressing than a graveyard. Feeling bored, she glanced at the motionless, frozen figures and suddenly her heart sank. Somehow she recognized one of the nuns – short, with thin shoulders and a black shawl on her head – as Olga, although when she had entered the convent she had been plump and taller, she thought. Deeply disturbed for some reason, Sophia Lvovna hesitantly walked over to the lay sister, looked over her shoulder into her face and saw it *was* Olga.

'Olga!' she said, clasping her hands and too excited to say anything else. 'Olga!'

The nun recognized her immediately, raised her eyebrows in astonishment and her pale, freshly washed face (even, it seemed, her white kerchief visible under her shawl) glowed with joy.

'God has performed a miracle,' she said and also clasped her thin, pale little hands.

Sophia Lvovna firmly embraced her and kissed her, frightened as she did so that her breath might smell of drink.

'We were just passing and we thought of you,' she said breathlessly, as though she had just completed a fast walk. 'Heavens, how pale you are! I'm . . . I'm very pleased to see you. Well, how are you? Bored?' Sophia Lvovna looked round at the other nuns and now she lowered her voice: 'So much has happened . . . you know I married Volodya Yagich. You must remember him . . . I'm very happy.'

'Well, thank the Lord for that! And is your father well?'

'Yes, he often remembers you. But you must come and see us during the holidays, Olga. Will you do that?'

'Yes, I'll come,' Olga said smiling. 'I'll come the day after tomorrow.'

Without even knowing why, Sophia burst into tears and cried in silence for a whole minute. Then she dried her eyes and said, 'Rita will be very sorry she didn't see you. She's with us too. And Little Volodya. They're at the gate. How pleased they would be to see you! Come out and see them, the service hasn't started yet.'

'All right,' Olga agreed. She crossed herself three times and walked out with Sophia Lvovna.

'So, you said you're happy, Sophia,' she said after they were past the gates.

'Very.'

'Well, thank God.'

When Big Volodya and Little Volodya saw the nun they got off the sledge and greeted her respectfully. They were visibly moved by her pale face and her nun's black habit, and they were both pleased that she remembered them and had come to greet them. Sophia Lvovna wrapped her in a rug and covered her with one flap of her fur coat to protect her from the cold. Her recent tears had lightened and cleansed her soul and she was glad that the noisy, riotous and essentially immoral night had unexpectedly come to such a pure and quiet conclusion. Then to keep Olga by her side longer, she suggested, 'Let's take her for a ride! Olga, get in. Just a little one.'

The men expected the nun to refuse – religious people don't go around in troikas – but to their amazement she agreed and got in. When the troika hurtled off towards the town gates, no one said a word; their only concern was to make her warm and comfortable. Each one of them thought about the difference in her from before. Her face was impassive, somewhat expressionless, cold, pale, transparent, as though water flowed in her veins instead of blood. Two or three years ago she had been buxom and rosy-cheeked, had talked about eligible bachelors and laughed loud at the least thing.

The troika turned round at the town gates. Ten minutes later they were back at the convent and Olga climbed out. The bells were ringing a series of chimes.

'God be with you,' Olga said, giving a low, nun-like bow.

'So you will come then, Olga?'

'Of course I will.'

She quickly left and soon disappeared through the dark gateway. After the troika had moved on everyone somehow felt very sad. No one said a word. Sophia Lvovna felt weak all over and her heart sank. Making a nun get into a sledge and go for a ride with that drunken crowd struck her now as stupid, tactless and almost sacrilegious. The desire for self-deception vanished with her tipsiness and now she clearly realized that she did not and could not love her husband, it was all nothing but silly nonsense. She had married for money because, as her ex-schoolgirl friends put it, he was 'madly rich', because she was terrified of becoming an old maid, like Rita, because her doctor father got on her nerves and because she wanted to annoy Little Volodya. Had she guessed when she was contemplating marriage that it would turn out to be so nasty, painful and ugly, she would never have agreed to it, not for anything in the world. But the damage was done now, she had to accept things.

They arrived home. As she lay in her warm, soft bed and covered herself with a blanket, Sophia Lvovna recalled the dark porch, the smell of incense, the figures by the columns, and she was distressed at the thought that these figures would still be standing there, quite motionless, all the time she was sleeping. Early morning service would be interminably long, and after that there would be the hours, then Mass, then more prayers . . .

'But surely God exists? He certainly exists and I must certainly die. Therefore, sooner or later, I must think of my soul, eternal life, like Olga does. Olga is saved now, she has solved all her problems for herself . . . But what if there is *no* God? Then her life has been wasted. But how has it been wasted? Why?'

A minute later another thought entered her head. 'God exists, death will certainly come. I should be thinking of my soul. If Olga could see her death this very minute she would not be afraid. She's ready. But the most important thing is, she's solved the riddle of existence for herself. God exists . . . yes. But isn't there another way out apart from becoming a nun? *That* means renouncing life, destroying it . . .' Sophia Lvovna became rather scared and hid her head under the pillow. 'I mustn't think about it,' she whispered, 'I mustn't.'

Yagich was walking up and down in the next room, his spurs softly jingling; he was deep in thought. Sophia Lvovna thought that this man was near and dear to her only in one thing – he was called Volodya too. She sat on her bed and tenderly called, 'Volodya!'

'What do you want?' her husband replied.

'Nothing.'

She lay down again. There were bells tolling – from that same convent, perhaps – and once again she recalled the porch and the dark figures. Thoughts of God and inescapable death wandered through her mind; she pulled the blanket over her head to drown the sound of the bells. She expected, before old age and death came, that her life would drag on for such a terribly long time, and from one day to the next she would have to cope with the nearness of someone she did not love, and who had come into the room just at that moment and was getting into bed; and she would have to suppress that hopeless love for another – someone who was so young, so charming and apparently so unusual. She looked at her husband and wanted to say good night, but she suddenly burst into tears instead. She felt annoyed with herself.

'Well, we're off again,' Yagich said.

She did calm down, but not until later, towards ten in the morning. She had stopped crying and shaking all over; she developed a severe headache, however. Yagich was hurrying, getting ready for late Mass and in the next room he was grumbling at the batman helping him dress. He came into the bedroom once, his spurs softly jingling, took something, and when he came in a second time he was wearing epaulettes and decorations; he limped slightly from rheumatism. He gave Sophia Lvovna the impression he was a beast of prey, prowling and looking round.

Then she heard him on the telephone. 'Please put me through to the Vasilyevsky Barracks,' he said. A minute later he went on, 'Is that Vasilyevsky Barracks? Please ask Dr Salimovich to come to the phone.' Then, a minute later, 'Who am I speaking to? Volodya? Fine. My dear chap, please ask your father to come over right away, my wife is terribly off colour after what happened yesterday. What's that? He's out? Hm . . . thanks . . . Yes, I'd be much obliged. *Merci*.'

Yagich came into the bedroom for the third time, bent over his wife, made the sign of the cross over her, let her kiss his hand (women who loved him would kiss his hand, he was used to this), and said he would be back for dinner. And he left.

Towards noon the maid announced Little Volodya. Swaying from weariness and her headache, Sophia Lvovna quickly put on her stunning new lilac, fur-trimmed negligee and hurriedly tidied her hair. In her heart she felt inexpressibly tender and trembled for joy – and for fear he might leave. She wanted just one look at him.

Little Volodya was paying her a visit in formal dress – tailcoat and white tie. When Sophia Lvovna came into the drawing-room he kissed her hand, said how deeply sorry he was to see her so unwell. When they had sat down he praised her negligee.

'Seeing Olga last night has upset me,' she said. 'At first it was painful for me, but now I envy her. She is like an immovable rock, it's impossible to budge her. But was there really no other way out for her, Volodya? Can burying oneself alive really solve life's problems? You'd call that death, not life, wouldn't you?' At the mention of Olga, Little Volodya's face showed deep emotion. 'Now look, Volodya, you're a clever man,' Sophia Lvovna said. 'Teach me to be like her. Of course, I'm a non-believer and I couldn't become a nun. But couldn't I do something that would be just as good? I find life hard enough.' After a brief silence she continued, 'Teach me . . . tell me something that will convince me. Just one word.'

'One word? Okay. Ta-ra-ra-boomdeay.'

'Volodya, why do you despise me?' she asked excitedly. 'You speak to me in some special – if you'll forgive the expression – fancy language that one doesn't use with friends and respectable women. You're a successful scholar, you love your studies, but why do you never tell me about them? Why? Aren't I good enough?'

Little Volodya frowned irritably and said, 'Why this sudden passion for scholarship? Perhaps you want us to have a constitution? Or perhaps sturgeon with horseradish?'

'Oh, have it your way then. I'm a mediocre, worthless, unprincipled, stupid woman . . . I've made thousands, thousands of mistakes. I'm not right in the head, a loose woman, and for that I deserve contempt. But you're ten years older than me, Volodya, aren't you? And my husband is thirty years older. You watched me grow up and if you'd wanted to, you could have made me anything you wanted, an angel even. But you . . .' (here her voice shook) 'treat me dreadfully. Yagich was an old man when he married me, and you . . .'

'Well, enough of that. Enough,' Volodya said, drawing closer to her and kissing both her hands. 'We'll leave the Schopenhauers to philosophize and argue about anything they like, but now we're going to kiss these sweet little hands.'

'You despise me and if only you knew the suffering it causes me,' she said hesitantly, knowing beforehand that he would not believe her. 'If you only knew how I want to improve myself, to start a new life! It fills me with joy just thinking about it,' she murmured and actually shed a few joyous tears. 'To be a good, honest, decent person, not to lie, to have a purpose in life.'

'Stop it please! You don't have to put on an act for me, I don't like it,' Volodya said, looking peevish. 'Heavens, you'd think we were at the theatre! Let's behave like normal human beings!'

To prevent him from leaving in a temper she began to make excuses, forced herself to smile – to please him – mentioned Olga again and that she wanted to solve the riddle of her existence, to become a real human being.

'Ta-ra-ra-boomdeay,' he chanted softly. 'Ta-ra-ra-boomdeay!'

And then quite suddenly he clasped her waist. Barely conscious of what she was doing she put her hands on his shoulders and for a whole minute looked rapturously at his clever, sarcastic face, his forehead, eyes, handsome beard . . .

'You've known for a long time that I love you,' she confessed with an agonized blush and she felt that even her lips had twisted in a paroxysm of shame. 'I love you. So why do you torment me?'

She closed her eyes and kissed him firmly on the lips. For a long time – a whole minute perhaps – she just could not bring herself to end this kiss, although she knew very well that she was behaving badly, that he might tell her off, or that a servant might come in . . .

Half an hour later, when he had got what he wanted, he sat in the dining-room eating a snack while she knelt before him, staring hungrily into his face. He told her she was like a small dog waiting for someone to toss it a piece of ham. Then he sat her on one knee, rocked her like a child and sang, 'Ta-ra-ra-boomdeay . . . Ta-ra-ra-boomdeay!'

When he was about to leave she asked him passionately, 'When? Later on? Where?' And she held out both hands to his mouth, as if wanting to catch his reply in them.

'It's not really convenient today,' he said after a moment's thought. 'Perhaps tomorrow, though.'

And they parted. Before lunch Sophia Lvovna went off to the convent to see Olga, but was told that she was reading the Psalter for someone who had died. From the convent she went to her father's and drove aimlessly up and down the main streets and side-streets until evening. While she was riding, for some reason she kept remembering that aunt with the tear-stained eyes, who was fretting her life away.

That night they all went riding on troikas again and heard the gypsies in that out-of-town restaurant. And when they were once again passing the convent Sophia Lvovna thought of Olga and became terrified at the thought that there was no escape for girls and women in her circle, except perpetual troika-rides or entering a convent to mortify the flesh . . .

The following day she had a lovers' rendezvous once again. She went for solitary cab-rides around town and thought of her aunt.

A week later Little Volodya dropped her. Then life reverted to normal and was just as boring, dreary – and sometimes just as excruciating as it had ever been. The Colonel and Little Volodya had long billiards and piquet sessions, Rita told her tasteless anecdotes in the same lifeless fashion,

Sophia Lvovna kept driving in cabs and asking her husband to take her for troika-rides.

Almost every day she called at the convent, boring Olga with her complaints of intolerable suffering; she cried and felt that she had brought something impure, pathetic and shabby into the cell. Olga, however, as if repeating a well-learnt lesson parrot-fashion, told her that there was nothing to worry about, that it would all pass and that God would forgive her.

Gooseberries

The sky had been overcast with rain clouds since early morning. The weather was mild, and not hot and oppressive as it can be on dull grey days when storm clouds lie over the fields for ages and you wait for rain which never comes. Ivan Ivanych, the vet, and Burkin, a teacher at the high school, were tired of walking and thought they would never come to the end of the fields. They could just make out the windmills at the village of Mironositskoye in the far distance – a range of hills stretched away to the right and disappeared far beyond it. They both knew that the river was there, with meadows, green willows and farmsteads, and that if they climbed one of the hills they would see yet another vast expanse of fields, telegraph wires and a train resembling a caterpillar in the distance. In fine weather they could see even as far as the town. And now, in calm weather, when the whole of nature had become gentle and dreamy, Ivan Ivanych and Burkin were filled with love for those open spaces and they both thought what a vast and beautiful country it was.

'Last time we were in Elder Prokofy's barn, you were going to tell me a story,' Burkin said.

'Yes, I wanted to tell you about my brother.'

Ivan Ivanych heaved a long sigh and lit his pipe before beginning his narrative; but at that moment down came the rain. Five minutes later it was simply teeming. Ivan Ivanych and Burkin were in two minds as to what they should do. The dogs were already soaked through and stood with their tails drooping, looking at them affectionately.

'We must take shelter,' Burkin said. 'Let's go to Alyokhin's, it's not very far.'

'All right, let's go there.'

They changed direction and went across mown fields, walking straight on at first, and then bearing right until they came out on the high road. Before long, poplars, a garden, then the red roofs of barns came into view. The river glinted, and then they caught sight of a wide stretch of water and a white bathing-hut. This was Sofino, where Alyokhin lived.

The mill was turning and drowned the noise of the rain. The wall of the dam shook. Wet horses with downcast heads were standing by some carts and peasants went around with sacks on their heads. Everything was damp, muddy and bleak, and the water had a cold, malevolent look. Ivan Ivanych and Burkin felt wet, dirty and terribly uncomfortable. Their feet were weighed down by mud and when they crossed the dam and walked up to the barns near the manor house they did not say a word and seemed to be angry with each other.

A winnowing fan was droning away in one of the barns and dust poured out of the open door. On the threshold stood the master himself, Alyokhin, a man of about forty, tall, stout, with long hair, and he looked more like a professor or an artist than a landowner. He wore a white shirt that hadn't been washed for a very long time, and it was tied round with a piece of rope as a belt. Instead of trousers he was wearing underpants; mud and straw clung to his boots. His nose and eyes were black with dust. He immediately recognized Ivan Ivanych and Burkin, and was clearly delighted to see them.

'Please come into the house, gentlemen,' he said, smiling, 'I'll be with you in a jiffy.'

It was a large house, with two storeys. Alyokhin lived on the ground floor in the two rooms with vaulted ceilings and small windows where his estate managers used to live. They were simply furnished and smelled of rye bread, cheap vodka and harness. He seldom used the main rooms upstairs, reserving them for guests. Ivan Ivanych and Burkin were welcomed by the maid, who was such a beautiful young woman that they both stopped and stared at each other.

'You can't imagine how glad I am to see you, gentlemen,' Alyokhin said as he followed them into the hall. 'A real surprise!' Then he turned to the maid and said, 'Pelageya, bring some dry clothes for the gentlemen. I suppose I'd better change too. But I must have a wash first, or you'll think I haven't had one since spring. Would you like to come to the bathing-hut while they get things ready in the house?'

The beautiful Pelageya, who had such a dainty look and gentle face, brought soap and towels, and Alyokhin went off with his guests to the bathing-hut.

'Yes, it's ages since I had a good wash,' he said as he undressed. 'As you can see, it's a nice hut. My father built it, but I never find time these days for a swim.'

He sat on one of the steps and smothered his long hair and neck with soap; the water turned brown.

'Yes, I must confess . . .' Ivan Ivanych muttered, with a meaningful look at his head.

'Haven't had a wash for ages,' Alyokhin repeated in his embarrassment and soaped himself again; the water turned a dark inky blue.

Ivan Ivanych came out of the cabin, dived in with a loud splash and swam in the rain, making broad sweeps with his arms and sending out waves with white lilies bobbing about on them. He swam right out to the middle of the reach and dived. A moment later he popped up somewhere else and swam on, continually trying to dive right to the bottom.

'Oh, good God,' he kept saying with great relish. 'Good God . . .'

He reached the mill, said a few words to the peasants, then he turned and floated on his back in the middle with his face under the rain. Burkin and Alyokhin were already dressed and ready to leave, but he kept on swimming and diving.

'Oh, dear God,' he said. 'Oh, God!'

'Now that's enough,' Burkin shouted.

They went back to the house. Only when the lamp in the large upstairs drawing-room was alight and Burkin and Ivan Ivanych, wearing silk dressing-gowns and warm slippers, were sitting in armchairs and Alyokhin, washed and combed now and with a new frock-coat on, was walking up and down, obviously savouring the warmth, cleanliness, dry clothes and light shoes, while his beautiful Pelageya glided silently over the carpet and gently smiled as she served tea and jam on a tray – only then did Ivan Ivanych begin his story. It seemed that Burkin and Alyokhin were not the only ones who were listening, but also the ladies (young and old) and the officers, who were looking down calmly and solemnly from their gilt frames on the walls.

'There are two of us brothers,' he began, 'myself – Ivan Ivanych – and Nikolay Ivanych, who's two years younger. I studied to be a vet, while Nikolay worked in the district tax office from the time he was nineteen. Chimsha-Gimalaysky, our father, had served as a private, but when he was promoted to officer we became hereditary gentlemen and owners of a small estate. After he died, this estate was sequestrated to pay off his debts, but despite this we spent our boyhood in the country free to do what we wanted. Just like any other village children, we stayed out in the fields and woods for days and nights, minded horses, stripped bark, went fishing, and so on . . . As you know very well, anyone who has ever caught a ruff or watched migrating thrushes swarming over his native village on cool clear autumn days can never live in a town afterwards and he'll always hanker after the free and open life until his dying day. My brother was miserable in the tax office. The years passed, but there he stayed, always at the same old desk, copying out the same old documents and obsessed with this longing for the country. And gradually this longing took the form of a definite wish, a dream of buying a nice little estate somewhere in the country, beside a river or a lake.

'He was a kind, gentle man and I was very fond of him, but I could never feel any sympathy for him in this longing to lock himself away in a country house for the rest of his life. They say a man needs only six feet of earth, but surely they must mean a corpse – not a *man*! These days they seem to think that it's very good if our educated classes want to go back to the land and set their hearts on a country estate. But in reality these estates are only that same six feet all over again. To leave the town and all its noise and hubbub, to go and shut yourself away on your little estate – that's no life! It's selfishness, laziness, a peculiar brand of monasticism that achieves nothing. A man needs more than six feet of earth and a little place in the country, he needs the whole wide world, the whole of nature, where there's room for him to display his potential, all the manifold attributes of his free spirit.

'As he sat there in his office, my brother Nikolay dreamt of soup made from his own home-grown cabbages, soup that would fill the whole house with a delicious smell; eating meals on the green grass; sleeping in the sun; sitting on a bench outside the main gates for hours on end and looking at the fields and woods. Booklets on agriculture and words of wisdom from calendars were his joy, his favourite spiritual nourishment. He liked newspapers as well, but he only read property adverts – for so many acres of arable land and meadows, with "house, river, garden, mill, and ponds fed by running springs". And he had visions of garden paths, flowers, fruit, nesting-boxes for starlings, ponds teeming with carp – you know the kind of thing. These visions varied according to the adverts he happened to see, but for some reason, in every single one, there *had* to be gooseberry bushes. "Life in the country has its comforts," he used to say. "You can sit drinking tea on your balcony, while your ducks are swimming in the pond . . . it all smells so good and um . . . there's your gooseberries growing away!"

'He drew up a plan for his estate and it turned out exactly

the same every time: (a) manor house; (b) servants' quarters; (c) kitchen garden; (d) gooseberry bushes. He lived a frugal life, economizing on food and drink, dressing any-old-how – just like a beggar – and putting every penny he saved straight into the bank. He was terribly mean. It was really painful to look at him, so I used to send him a little money on special occasions. But he would put that in the bank too. Once a man has his mind firmly made up there's nothing you can do about it.

'Years passed and he was transferred to another province. He was now in his forties, still reading newspaper adverts and still saving up. Then I heard that he'd got married. So that he could buy a country estate with gooseberry bushes, he married an ugly old widow, for whom he felt nothing and only because she had a little money tucked away. He made her life miserable too, half-starved her and banked her money into his own account. She'd been married to a postmaster and was used to pies and fruit liqueurs, but with her second husband she didn't even have enough black bread. This kind of life made her wither away, and within three years she'd gone to join her maker. Of course, my brother didn't think that *he* was to blame – not for one minute! Like vodka, money can make a man do the most peculiar things. There was once a merchant living in our town who was on his deathbed. Just before he died, he asked for some honey, stirred it up with all his money and winning lottery tickets, and swallowed the lot to stop anyone else from laying their hands on it. And another time, when I was inspecting cattle at some railway station, a dealer fell under a train and had his leg cut off. We took him to the local casualty department.

The blood simply gushed out, a terrible sight, but all he did was ask for his leg back and was only bothered about the twenty roubles he had tucked away in the boot. Scared he might lose them, I dare say!'

'But that's neither here nor there,' Burkin said.

'When his wife died,' Ivan continued, after a pause for thought, 'my brother started looking for an estate. Of course, you can look around for five years and still make the wrong choice and you finish up with something you never even dreamt of. So brother Nikolay bought about three hundred acres, with manor house, servants' quarters and a park, on a mortgage through an estate agent. But there wasn't any orchard, gooseberries or duck pond. There *was* a river, but the water was always the colour of coffee because of the brickworks on one side of the estate and a bone-ash factory on the other. But my dear Nikolay didn't seem to care. He ordered twenty gooseberry bushes, planted them out and settled down to a landowner's life.

'Last year I visited him, as I wanted to see what was going on. In his letter my brother had called his estate "Chumbaroklov Patch" or "Gimalaysky's". One afternoon I turned up at "Gimalaysky's". It was a hot day. Everywhere there were ditches, fences, hedges, rows of small fir trees and there seemed no way into the yard or anywhere to leave my horse. I went up to the house, only to be welcomed by a fat ginger dog that looked rather like a pig. It wanted to bark, but it was too lazy. Then a barefooted, plump cook – she resembled a pig as well – came out of the kitchen and told me the master was having his after-lunch nap. So I went to my brother's room and there he was sitting up in bed with a blanket over his knees. He'd aged, put on weight and looked very flabby. His cheeks, nose and lips stuck out and I thought any moment he was going to grunt into his blanket, like a pig.

'We embraced and wept for joy, and at the sad thought that once we were young and now both of us were grey, and that our lives were nearly over. He got dressed and led me on a tour of the estate.

' "Well, how's it going?" I asked.

' "All right, thank God. It's a good life."

'No longer was he the poor, timid little clerk of before, but a real squire, a *gentleman*. He felt quite at home, being used to country life by then and he was enjoying himself. He ate a great deal, took proper baths, and he was putting on weight. Already he was suing the district council and both factories, and he got very peeved when the villagers didn't call him "sir". He paid great attention to his spiritual well-being (as a gentleman should) and he couldn't dispense charity nice and quietly, but had to make a great show of it. And what did it all add up to? He doled out bicarbonate of soda or castor oil to his villagers – regardless of what they were suffering from – and on his name-day held a thanksgiving service in the village, supplying vodka in plenty, as he thought this was the right thing to do. Oh, those horrid pints of vodka! Nowadays your fat squire drags his villagers off to court for letting their cattle stray on his land and the very next day (if it's a high holiday) stands them all a few pints of vodka. They'll drink it, shout hurray and fall at his feet in a drunken stupor. Better standards of living, plenty to eat, idleness – all this makes us Russians terribly smug. Back in his office, Nikolay had been too scared even to voice any opinions of his own, but now he was expounding the eternal verities in true ministerial style: "Education is essential, but premature as far as the common people are concerned" or "Corporal punishment, generally speaking, is harmful, but in certain cases it can be useful and irreplaceable". And he'd say, "I know the working classes and how to handle them. They *like* me, I only have to lift my little finger and they'll do *anything* for me."

'And he said all this, mark you, with a clever, good-natured smile. Time after time he'd say "we *gentlemen*" or "speaking as *one of the gentry*". He'd evidently forgotten that our grandfather had been a peasant and our father a common soldier. Even our absolutely ridiculous surname, Chimsha-Gimalaysky, was melodious, distinguished and highly agreeable to his ears now.

'But it's myself I'm concerned with, not him. I'd like to tell you about the change that came over me during the few hours I spent on his estate. Later, when we were having tea, his cook brought us a plateful of gooseberries. They weren't shop gooseberries, but home-grown, the first fruits of the bushes he'd planted. Nikolay laughed and stared at them for a whole minute, with tears in his eyes. He was too deeply moved for words. Then he popped one in his mouth, looked at me like an enraptured child that has finally been given a long-awaited toy and said, "Absolutely delicious!" He ate some greedily and kept repeating, "So tasty, you *must* try one!"

'They were hard and sour, but as Pushkin says: "Uplifting illusion is dearer to us than a host of truths." This was a happy man whose cherished dreams had clearly come true, who had achieved his life's purpose, had got what he wanted and was happy with his lot – and himself. My thoughts about human happiness, for some peculiar reason, had always been tinged with a certain sadness. But now, seeing this happy man, I was overwhelmed by a feeling of despondency that was close to utter despair. I felt particularly low that night. They made up a bed for me in the room next to my brother's. He was wide awake and I could hear him getting up, going over to the plate and helping himself to one gooseberry at a time. And I thought how many satisfied, happy people really do exist in this world! And what a powerful force they are! Just take a look at this life of ours and you will see the arrogance and idleness of the strong, the ignorance and bestiality of the weak. Everywhere there's unspeakable poverty, overcrowding, degeneracy, drunkenness, hypocrisy and stupid lies . . . And yet peace and quiet reign in every house and street. Out of fifty thousand people you won't find one who is prepared to shout out loud and make a strong protest. We see people buying food in the market, eating during the day, sleeping at night-time, talking nonsense, marrying, growing old and then contentedly carting their dead off to the cemetery. But we don't hear or see those who suffer: the real tragedies of life are enacted somewhere behind the scenes. Everything is calm and peaceful and the only protest comes from statistics – and they can't talk. Figures show that so many went mad, so many bottles of vodka were emptied, so many children died from malnutrition. And clearly this kind of system is what people need. It's obvious that the happy man feels contented only because the unhappy ones bear their burden without saying a word: if it weren't for their silence, happiness would be quite impossible. It's a kind of mass hypnosis. Someone ought to stand with a hammer at the door of every happy contented man, continually banging on it to remind him that there are unhappy people around and that however happy *he* may be at the time, sooner or later life will show him its claws and disaster will overtake him in the form of illness, poverty, bereavement and there will be no one to hear or see him. But there isn't anyone holding a hammer, so our happy man goes his own sweet way and is only gently ruffled by life's trivial cares, as an aspen is ruffled by the breeze. All's well as far as *he's* concerned.

'That night I realized that I too was happy and contented,' Ivan Ivanych went on, getting to his feet. 'I too had lectured people over dinner – or out hunting – on how to live, on what to believe, on how to handle the common people. And I too had told them that knowledge is a shining lamp, that education is essential, and that plain reading and writing is good enough for the masses, for the moment. Freedom is a blessing, I told them, and we need it like the air we breathe, but we must wait for it patiently.'

Ivan Ivanych turned to Burkin and said angrily, 'Yes, that's what I used to say and now I'd like to know *what* is it we're waiting for? I'm asking you, *what*? What is it we're trying to prove? I'm told that nothing can be achieved in five minutes, that it takes time for any kind of idea to be realized; it's a gradual process. But who says so? And what is there to prove he's right? You refer to the natural order of things, to the law of cause and effect. But *is* there any law or order in a state of affairs where a lively, thinking person like myself should have to stand by a ditch and wait until it's choked with weeds, or silted up, when I could quite easily, perhaps, leap across it or bridge it? I ask you again, what are we waiting for? Until we have no more strength to live, although we long to and *need* to go on living?

'I left my brother early next morning and ever since then I've found town life unbearable. I'm depressed by peace and quiet, I'm scared of peering through windows, nothing makes me more dejected than the sight of a happy family sitting round the table drinking tea. But I'm old now, no longer fit for the fray, I'm even incapable of hating. I only feel sick at heart, irritable and exasperated. At night my head seems to be on fire with so many thoughts crowding in and I can't get any sleep . . . Oh, if only I were young again!'

Ivan Ivanych paced the room excitedly, repeating, 'If only I were young again!'

Suddenly he went up to Alyokhin and squeezed one hand, then the other. 'Pavel Konstantinych,' he pleaded, 'don't go to sleep or be lulled into complacency! While you're still young, strong and healthy, never stop doing good! Happiness doesn't exist, we don't need any such thing. If life has *any* meaning or purpose, you won't find it in happiness, but in something more rational, in something greater. Doing good!'

Ivan Ivanych said all this with a pitiful, imploring smile, as though pleading for himself.

Afterwards all three of them sat in armchairs in different parts of the room and said nothing. Ivan Ivanych's story satisfied neither Burkin nor Alyokhin. It was boring listening to that story about some poor devil of a clerk who ate gooseberries, while those generals and ladies, who seemed to have come to life in the gathering gloom, peered out of their gilt frames. For some reason they would have preferred discussing and hearing about refined people, about ladies. The fact that they were all sitting in a drawing-room where everything – the draped chandeliers, the armchairs, the carpets underfoot – indicated that those same people who were now looking out of their frames had once walked around, sat down and drunk their tea there . . . and with beautiful Pelageya moving about here without a sound – all this was better than any story.

Alyokhin was dying to get to bed. That morning he had been up and about very early (before three) working on the farm, and he could hardly keep his eyes open. However, he was frightened he might miss some interesting story if he left now, so he stayed. He didn't even try to fathom if everything that Ivan Ivanych had just been saying was clever, or even true: he was only too glad that his guests did not discuss oats or hay or tar, but things that had nothing to do with his way of life, and he wanted them to continue . . .

'But it's time we got some sleep,' Burkin said, standing up. 'May I wish you all a very good night!'

Alyokhin bade them good night and went down to his room, while his guests stayed upstairs. They had been given the large room with two old, elaborately carved beds and an ivory crucifix in one corner. These wide, cool beds had been made by the beautiful Pelageya and the linen had a pleasant fresh smell.

Ivan Ivanych undressed without a word and got into bed.

Then he muttered, 'Lord have mercy on us sinners!' and pulled the blankets over his head. His pipe, which was lying on a table, smelt strongly of stale tobacco and Burkin was so puzzled as to where the terrible smell was coming from that it was a long time before he fell asleep.

All night long the rain beat against the windows.

1. BOCCACCIO · *Mrs Rosie and the Priest*
2. GERARD MANLEY HOPKINS · *As kingfishers catch fire*
3. *The Saga of Gunnlaug Serpent-tongue*
4. THOMAS DE QUINCEY · *On Murder Considered as One of the Fine Arts*
5. FRIEDRICH NIETZSCHE · *Aphorisms on Love and Hate*
6. JOHN RUSKIN · *Traffic*
7. PU SONGLING · *Wailing Ghosts*
8. JONATHAN SWIFT · *A Modest Proposal*
9. *Three Tang Dynasty Poets*
10. WALT WHITMAN · *On the Beach at Night Alone*
11. KENKŌ · *A Cup of Sake Beneath the Cherry Trees*
12. BALTASAR GRACIÁN · *How to Use Your Enemies*
13. JOHN KEATS · *The Eve of St Agnes*
14. THOMAS HARDY · *Woman much missed*
15. GUY DE MAUPASSANT · *Femme Fatale*
16. MARCO POLO · *Travels in the Land of Serpents and Pearls*
17. SUETONIUS · *Caligula*
18. APOLLONIUS OF RHODES · *Jason and Medea*
19. ROBERT LOUIS STEVENSON · *Olalla*
20. KARL MARX AND FRIEDRICH ENGELS · *The Communist Manifesto*
21. PETRONIUS · *Trimalchio's Feast*
22. JOHANN PETER HEBEL · *How a Ghastly Story Was Brought to Light by a Common or Garden Butcher's Dog*
23. HANS CHRISTIAN ANDERSEN · *The Tinder Box*
24. RUDYARD KIPLING · *The Gate of the Hundred Sorrows*
25. DANTE · *Circles of Hell*
26. HENRY MAYHEW · *Of Street Piemen*
27. HAFEZ · *The nightingales are drunk*
28. GEOFFREY CHAUCER · *The Wife of Bath*
29. MICHEL DE MONTAIGNE · *How We Weep and Laugh at the Same Thing*
30. THOMAS NASHE · *The Terrors of the Night*
31. EDGAR ALLAN POE · *The Tell-Tale Heart*
32. MARY KINGSLEY · *A Hippo Banquet*
33. JANE AUSTEN · *The Beautifull Cassandra*
34. ANTON CHEKHOV · *Gooseberries*
35. SAMUEL TAYLOR COLERIDGE · *Well, they are gone, and here must I remain*
36. JOHANN WOLFGANG VON GOETHE · *Sketchy, Doubtful, Incomplete Jottings*
37. CHARLES DICKENS · *The Great Winglebury Duel*
38. HERMAN MELVILLE · *The Maldive Shark*
39. ELIZABETH GASKELL · *The Old Nurse's Story*
40. NIKOLAY LESKOV · *The Steel Flea*

41. HONORÉ DE BALZAC · *The Atheist's Mass*
42. CHARLOTTE PERKINS GILMAN · *The Yellow Wall-Paper*
43. C.P. CAVAFY · *Remember, Body . . .*
44. FYODOR DOSTOEVSKY · *The Meek One*
45. GUSTAVE FLAUBERT · *A Simple Heart*
46. NIKOLAI GOGOL · *The Nose*
47. SAMUEL PEPYS · *The Great Fire of London*
48. EDITH WHARTON · *The Reckoning*
49. HENRY JAMES · *The Figure in the Carpet*
50. WILFRED OWEN · *Anthem For Doomed Youth*
51. WOLFGANG AMADEUS MOZART · *My Dearest Father*
52. PLATO · *Socrates' Defence*
53. CHRISTINA ROSSETTI · *Goblin Market*
54. *Sindbad the Sailor*
55. SOPHOCLES · *Antigone*
56. RYŪNOSUKE AKUTAGAWA · *The Life of a Stupid Man*
57. LEO TOLSTOY · *How Much Land Does A Man Need?*
58. GIORGIO VASARI · *Leonardo da Vinci*
59. OSCAR WILDE · *Lord Arthur Savile's Crime*
60. SHEN FU · *The Old Man of the Moon*
61. AESOP · *The Dolphins, the Whales and the Gudgeon*
62. MATSUO BASHŌ · *Lips too Chilled*
63. EMILY BRONTË · *The Night is Darkening Round Me*
64. JOSEPH CONRAD · *To-morrow*
65. RICHARD HAKLUYT · *The Voyage of Sir Francis Drake Around the Whole Globe*
66. KATE CHOPIN · *A Pair of Silk Stockings*
67. CHARLES DARWIN · *It was snowing butterflies*
68. BROTHERS GRIMM · *The Robber Bridegroom*
69. CATULLUS · *I Hate and I Love*
70. HOMER · *Circe and the Cyclops*
71. D. H. LAWRENCE · *Il Duro*
72. KATHERINE MANSFIELD · *Miss Brill*
73. OVID · *The Fall of Icarus*
74. SAPPHO · *Come Close*
75. IVAN TURGENEV · *Kasyan from the Beautiful Lands*
76. VIRGIL · *O Cruel Alexis*
77. H. G. WELLS · *A Slip under the Microscope*
78. HERODOTUS · *The Madness of Cambyses*
79. *Speaking of Siva*
80. *The Dhammapada*